## *Dear Parent:*
## *Your child's love of readin*

Every child learns to read in a different way and at his or her own speed. Some go back and forth between reading levels and read favorite books again and again. Others read through each level in order. You can help your young reader improve and become more confident by encouraging his or her own interests and abilities. From books your child reads with you to the first books he or she reads alone, there are I Can Read Books for every stage of reading:

**SHARED READING**
Basic language, word repetition, and whimsical illustrations, ideal for sharing with your emergent reader

**BEGINNING READING**
Short sentences, familiar words, and simple concepts for children eager to read on their own

**READING WITH HELP**
Engaging stories, longer sentences, and language play for developing readers

**READING ALONE**
Complex plots, challenging vocabulary, and high-interest topics for the independent reader

**ADVANCED READING**
Short paragraphs, chapters, and exciting themes for the perfect bridge to chapter books

**I Can Read Books** have introduced children to the joy of reading since 1957. Featuring award-winning authors and illustrators and a fabulous cast of beloved characters, I Can Read Books set the standard for beginning readers.

A lifetime of discovery begins with the magical words **"I Can Read!"**

*Visit www.icanread.com for information on enriching your child's reading experience.*

 For information address HarperCollins Children's Books, a division of HarperCollins Publishers, 10 East 53rd Street, New York, NY 10022.
www.icanread.com

Library of Congress catalog card number: 2009938846
ISBN 978-0-06-168971-0 (trade bdg.) —ISBN 978-0-06-057418-5 (pbk.)

10 11 12 13 14 SCP 10 9 8 7 6 5 4 3 2 1 ❖ First Edition

# The Berenstain Bears
# ALL ABOARD!

Jan and Mike Berenstain

**HARPER**
*An Imprint of* Harper Collins*Publishers*

Grizzlyville
CKETS

The Bear family is going on a trip.

They are visiting their aunt Tillie.

To get there, they will catch a train.

Brother and Sister look down the track.

Here comes the train!

"*WOO-HOO!*"

goes the whistle.

The train comes into the station.

It is pulled by a big, shiny engine.

Clouds of smoke puff out of the smokestack.

It makes a lot of noise!

Brother, Sister, and Honey Bear cover their ears.

88
BEAR COUNTRY
EXPRESS

Someone waves from the train.

It is Grizzly Jones, the engineer.

He drives the train.

Mr. Mack is the conductor.

He makes sure the train leaves on time.

"All aboard!" he calls.

The family finds their seats.
The train starts with a jerk.
Honey Bear thinks that is funny.
Mr. Mack takes their tickets.

At first they go slow.

Then they go faster.

They pass their tree house.

They pass Farmer Ben's Farm.

Farmer Ben waves from his tractor.

The Bear Country School
TOWN HALL
GROCERY

They pass the Bear Country School.

Handy bear Gus is fixing the roof.

They go through Grizzlyville.

They see cars and streetlights.

They see stores and traffic cops.

The train crosses a bridge.

They see bears in boats fishing.

They see bears working on the railroad.

They go through a tunnel.

BC
RR

The train climbs into the mountains.

They pass bears skiing and climbing.

The train goes down in a valley.

They see mountain goats and deer.

B

The cubs get tired of looking
out the window.
Mr. Mack asks if they want to
visit the engine.
Grizzly Jones is driving.
His helper throws coal on the fire
to make the train go.

Grizzly lets them blow the whistle.
"*WOO-HOO!*" goes the whistle.
"Would you like to drive the train?"
asks Grizzly Jones.
Would they ever!
The cubs take turns
in the driver's seat.

88
BEAR COUNTRY
EXPRESS

A freight train comes along.

At the end there is a red caboose.

It is like a little house on wheels.

The train's conductor lives there.

He waves as they go past.

The cubs go back to their seats.

They are getting hungry.

Mama has a lunch basket.

The Bears eat as the train

rolls on.

Soon, the train slows down.

They pull into a station.

The train stops and gives off

a big puff of steam.

"*Whoosh!*"

Good-bye, Mr. Mack and Grizzly Jones.

The cubs enjoyed their ride on the train.

Beartown

Aunt Tillie is waiting in her car.

"I want to be an engineer when I grow up," Sister says.

"What about you, Brother?" asks Aunt Tillie.

"I want to live in a red caboose!" he says.

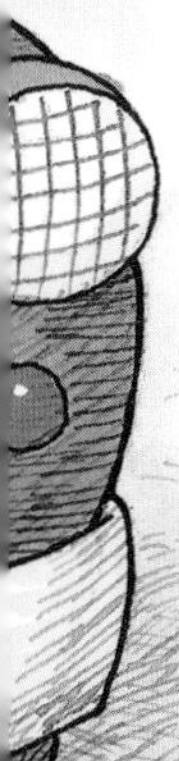

“So do I,” says Aunt Tillie.